DARE TO REPAIR!

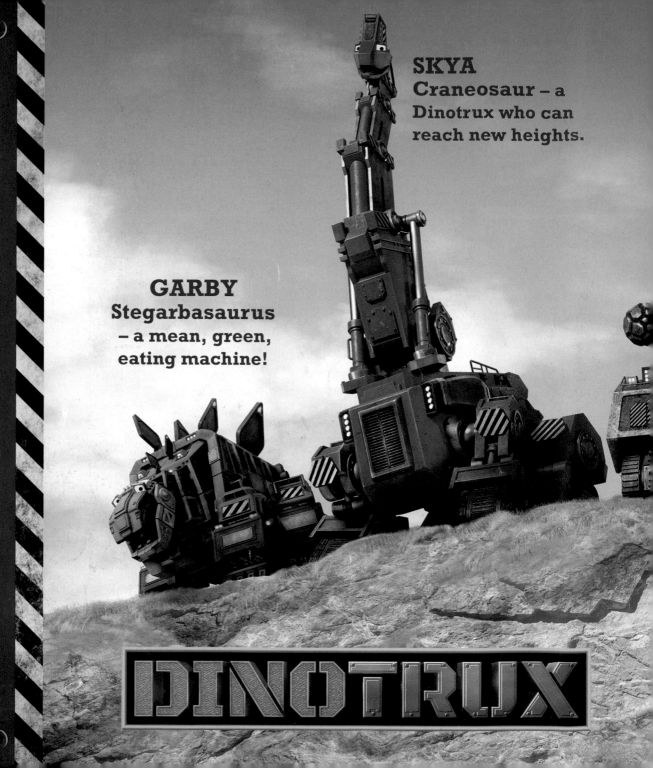

SKYA
Craneosaur – a Dinotrux who can reach new heights.

GARBY
Stegarbasaurus – a mean, green, eating machine!

DINOTRUX

TY RUX
Tyrannosaurus Trux –
the leader of the team!

DOZER
Dozeratops – has
a heart as big as his
Dozeratops blade.

TON-TON
Anklyodump –
always ready
for action!

REVVIT
Rotilian Reptool
– Ty's best friend.

Revvit was busy finishing up a repair job on his new friend Ty.

"Thanks Revvit!" Ty cheered, all fixed.

When the other Dinotrux saw Revvit's work, they wanted him to fix them, too.

"Think you can help us, dude?" Ton-Ton asked.

"Maybe," replied Revvit. "But I can't do it alone."

Revvit rushed back to the ravine. The other Reptools came out to meet him.

"Where have you been?" asked Click-Clack. "It's dangerous outside."

"I found some new friends!" announced Revvit. "And they need our help. Follow me."

Revvit led his nervous friends out to the crater. Little Reptools and dangerous Dinotrux did not mix!

A huge mechanical creature rolled out of the shadows.

"Aaaaah!" screamed the Reptools.

"This T-Trux is not going to hurt us," said Revvit. "He's my friend, Ty. And right now, he needs our help."

"How could Reptools possibly help Dinotrux?" gasped Ace.

"By repairing them, of course!" said Revvit.

Ace's eyes lit up.

"You mean, we could actually work on them?" she asked.

"Yes!" grinned Revvit. "Do you want to return to the ravine or do you want to start living big?"

The Reptools agreed excitedly. They wanted to live big and work on the huge Dinotrux.

The Reptools got to work.
  "I still don't think we should be
out in the open like this,"
worried Waldo.
  "We're Dinotrux!" smiled Ty.
"Nothing can happen with us around."

Suddenly, a group of Scrapadactyls swooped down from the
sky and grabbed the little Reptools.
  "We must protect our friends!" thundered Ty.
  But the Scrapadactyls were too fast.

"It looks like they are headed towards those cliffs," shouted Ty. "Who's coming with me?"

"We're in!" shouted the Dinotrux together.
"Come on," Dozer rumbled. "Let's do this!"

The Scrapadactyls dropped the Reptools into their nest at the very top of a huge pile of rocks. Far down below, the Dinotrux revved their engines.

"Don't worry, Reptools!" called Ty. "We'll get you out of there!"

The Dinotrux gave it their best shot, but even Dozer couldn't knock the nest down!

"We need a new plan." Ty groaned. "This is tougher than I thought"

Then he had an idea.

He picked up a scrap of metal and tossed it toward the Scrapadactyls.

"You want more scrap?" he asked. "Go get it!"

"He's trying to lure them away from the nest," gasped Skya. "Let's help!"

The Dinotrux threw the scrap further and further away.

And soon the Scrapadactyls had flown away from the nest.

When they had all disappeared, the Dinotrux worked together to rescue the Reptools.

"Thanks for saving us!" said Waldo. "But those Scrapadactyls will come back one day, and I don't want to be here when they do."

Ace agreed. "There's a reason why we Reptools live in the ravine. It's a protected place."

"A protected place ..." mumbled Ty.
"Are you thinking what I'm thinking?" asked Revvit.
Ty nodded and they began to make a plan.

The Reptools went home to the safe ravine. But now it seemed too quiet without their new friends.

A little while later Revvit appeared.

"I know you all loved fixing those Trux," he said. "What if there was somewhere we could be safe while doing our repairs?"

"Somewhere like the ravine?" asked Waldo
"But big enough for the Dinotrux ..." added Click-Clack.

"Exactly!" grinned Revvit, showing the Reptools his plans.

"Ty and I are going to work together and build a garage big enough for all the Dinotrux." Revvit proudly said. "And we'll all be able to work there safely together!"